Wilberforce

Goes Shopping

Margaret Gordon

Puffin Books

One day Wilberforce went downstairs,

to find Grandfather and Grandmother.

Grandfather had finished the washing-up.

Grandmother was making a shopping list.

Grandfather found the shopping bags.

Grandmother shut the larder.

Wilberforce said goodbye to Mother,

waved to Baby and went off to the shops.

They went past the swings to the supermarket,

and Grandfather went to the butcher's.

They needed some baked beans.

Wilberforce found them,

and carefully

took out the best can.

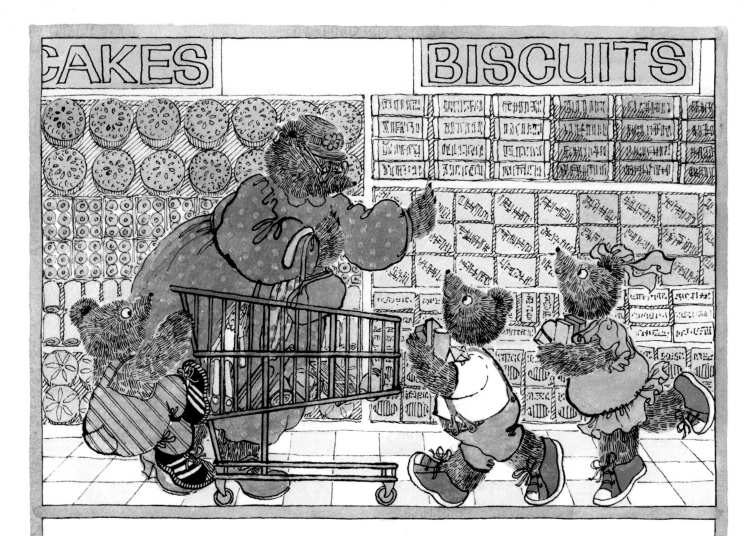

Grandmother filled up the trolley,

and Wilberforce . . .

took it to the checkout.

They kept Grandfather out of the baker's.

Grandmother bought bread and seven cakes.

Grandfather collected the shopping bags.

They were very heavy,

and everybody helped to carry them.

They went back, past the swings,

up the street and home.

Grandfather unpacked the shopping.

Grandmother made the tea.

Mother and Baby came to have some too.

Then Wilberforce went upstairs to play.